PHANTOM OF THE LIBRARY

STONE ARCH BOOKS

a capstone imprint

SNOOPS, INC. IS PUBLISHED BY
STONE ARCH BOOKS, A CAPSTONE IMPRINT
1710 ROE CREST DRIVE
NORTH MANKATO, MINNESOTA 56003
WWW.MYCAPSTONE.COM

Library of Congress Cataloging-in-Publication Data
Names: Terrell, Brandon, 1978– author. | Epelbaum, Mariano, 1975– illustrator. |
Terrell, Brandon, 1978– Snoops, Inc.
Title: Phantom of the library / by Brandon Terrell ; illustrated by Mariano Epelbaum.
Description: North Mankato, Minnesota : Stone Arch Books, a Capstone imprint, [2018]
| Series: Snoops, inc.
Identifiers: LCCN 2017002465 (print) | LCCN 2017005200 (ebook) |
ISBN 9781496550606 (library binding) | ISBN 9781496550620 (paperback) |
ISBN 9781496550644 (eBook PDF)
Subjects: LCSH: Public libraries—Juvenile fiction. | Theft—Juvenile fiction. |
Video recording—Juvenile fiction. | Twins—Juvenile fiction. | Brothers and sisters—
Juvenile fiction. | Friendship—Juvenile fiction. | Detective and mystery stories. |
CYAC: Mystery and detective stories. | Libraries—Fiction. | Stealing—Fiction. |
Internet television—Fiction. | Twins—Fiction. | Brothers and sisters—Fiction. |
Friendship—Fiction. | GSAFD: Mystery fiction. | LCGFT: Detective and mystery fiction.
Classification: LCC PZ7.T273 Ph 2018 (print) | LCC PZ7.T273 (ebook) |
DDC 813.6 [Fic]—dc23
LC record available at https://lccn.loc.gov/2017002465
Design elements: Shutterstock: In-Finity, loftystyle, veronchick84

BY BRANDON TERRELL

**ILLUSTRATED BY
MARIANO EPELBAUM**

EDITED BY: AARON SAUTTER
BOOK DESIGN BY: TED WILLIAMS
PRODUCTION BY: KATHY MCCOLLEY

SNOOPS INC.

ZIPPY 'ZA

PETS GALORE

HENSON PARK

DIAZ
GROCERIES

FLEISCHMAN
MIDDLE SCHOOL

PENDLETON
PUBLIC LIBRARY

BURGER BOOM!

THE COMIC
VAULT

SNOOPS HQ

CHAPTER 1

THE BIG CHEAT

Twelve-year-old Jaden Williams had never been afraid of walking into a bathroom before. He stood in the empty hallway in the abandoned section of Fleischman Middle School. The run-down brick walls were in need of repair, and the area had been closed to students the entire school year.

The bathroom door in front of him had a sign taped to it that read: Out of Order. The lights in the hall were off, casting the area in shadow.

But it wasn't the darkness and emptiness that freaked Jaden out.

It was the person waiting on the other side of the door.

He was a legend. A ghost. His name was whispered by kids who didn't study for their tests. For the right price, the answers to a test or a quiz — or a copy of a perfectly written research paper — could be yours.

And Jaden was meeting the legend right now. Well, as soon as he mustered up the courage to push open the door.

Jaden exhaled long and slow. "You can do this," he whispered to himself. Then he adjusted his baseball cap so the brim almost covered his eyes. The door moaned as it opened like a butler announcing the entrance of a new guest.

At first, Jaden couldn't see much in the dim light of the bathroom. The window high in the wall was cracked open. That was good. There was a row of sinks and a narrow, dusty mirror that someone had drawn a smiley face on with their finger. Across from the mirrors was a row of toilet stalls — and a pair of large black boots in the closest one.

Jaden gulped.

"H-hello?" he managed to squeak out. "I'm looking to b-b-buy a test . . ."

For a moment, nothing happened. Jaden watched the pair of boots. Finally, after what felt like forever, they began to move.

This is a bad idea, he repeated over and over in his head.

The stall door opened, and the kid wearing the large black boots stepped out.

Jaden's face screwed up in a look of shock and confusion.

The boy was short and skinny, not at all the huge, Paul Bunyan–like giant Jaden had imagined he'd be meeting. His boots looked comically large. A pair of thick-rimmed glasses perched low on his nose. He used one finger to push them back into place, his eyes never leaving Jaden.

Jaden didn't recognize the boy. *Carlos was right*, Jaden thought. *Big Boots must be another eighth-grader.* That's why Jaden had been sent in to meet the cheater instead of another member of their gumshoe detective crew. Jaden was a sixth-grader, so it was doubtful the older boy would recognize him.

Jaden felt Big Boots' piercing gaze. Despite his small size, Jaden was still intimidated by him.

"It's . . . cool," Jaden yammered. "I mean, I'm . . . heh . . . I'm not wearing a wire or anything." He laughed nervously, patting his chest to prove his point.

Big Boots said nothing . . .

"You've got to be kidding me," Hayden said to herself. Jaden's twin sister sat in one of the trees lining the sidewalk outside the school. With one hand, she clutched the tree trunk. With the other she held a strange-looking device she'd built earlier that day. It was a video game controller shaped like a sci-fi blaster with an old, clear-plastic bowl glued to one end of it. A microphone was attached to the controller inside the dish. A cord ran through the controller and into Hayden's phone. Thirteen-year-old Keisha Turner stood at the base of the tree. The seventh-grade girl craned her neck up to look at Hayden. "Is your microphone picking anything up?" she asked.

"Just my brother almost blowing our operation," Hayden whispered. She pointed the microphone at the window and hit record on her phone. Because of the shape of the dish, the microphone could pick up the conversation inside the old bathroom . . .

. . . where Jaden stood frozen in fear, having — and losing — a staring contest with Big Boots.

"Um, everything okay?" Jaden asked.

Slowly, Boots nodded. "Follow me," he said in a nasally voice.

Boots led Jaden to the last stall by the open window. Jaden hoped his sister was just outside and that this little operation was almost over.

Boots stepped into the stall and lifted the tank lid off the stall's toilet. Inside, instead of water, was a computer tablet. "What do you need? Mrs. Jamieson's pop quiz? Mr. Lin's multiple choice?"

"Yeah. Um, that one."

Boots looked over his glasses at Jaden. "Which one?"

"The . . . the multiple choice."

Boots silently tapped his fingers on the screen. Then he took a small USB drive from his pocket, plugged it into the tablet, and popped it back out a moment later.

"Here ya go," he said as Jaden took the device. "You'll get one day with the drive before it erases itself. Then poof, the test is gone, and the drive is worthless. So study up."

"Do I, uh, . . . pay you now?" Jaden reached into his pocket like he was digging for money.

"That's usually how this works," Boots said.

"Cool. In that case," Jaden raised his voice. "Cue ball in the corner pocket."

12

In the tree outside, Hayden whispered, "That's it! We've got what we need! Time to send in Carlos!"

Keisha relayed the message to Carlos on her phone.

Boots took a step toward Jaden. "What did you say?"

Even though Jaden was a good six inches taller, he stepped back.

"CUE BALL IN THE CORNER POCKET!" Jaden shouted at the top of his lungs.

The bathroom door burst open to reveal Carlos Diaz, the fourteen-year-old leader of Snoops, Inc. Carlos wore a wide smile; he loved solving mysteries and busting crooks more than anything in the world.

Right behind Carlos was the imposing principal of Fleischman Middle School. Principal Snider's face scowled, and his bald head gleamed in the dim bathroom light. Snider's muscular arms were folded across his big, barrel-like chest.

"Well, if it isn't Eugene Fairbanks," Principal Snider said disapprovingly. "Looks like your cheating days are over."

Now it was Boots' turn to look scared.

"Jeez," Jaden said to Carlos, "What took you so long?"

Rushing into the bathroom, out of breath, came Keisha and Hayden. Hayden carried her makeshift microphone like a futuristic space laser gun. A small twig stuck out of her hair.

"Are we in time? Did we miss the best part?" Hayden wheezed.

"Nope," Carlos said.

"Can I say it?" Jaden asked. "Please?"

Carlos sighed. "Fine."

Smiling, Jaden said, "Looks like you've been busted by Snoops, Incorporated."

"And by one angry principal," Principal Snider added sternly.

CHAPTER 2

A PRICELESS DISPLAY

The following evening, as the four Snoops walked toward their destination — Pendleton Public Library — they saw storefronts and homes decorated for Halloween. Jack-o'-lanterns sat grinning on doorsteps. Fake skeletons hung in windows. The crisp fall air was brisk and refreshing. Every bit of it made Carlos smile. He absolutely loved this time of year.

Their adventure for the night excited him.
It didn't involve the usual bike thieves or
shoplifters. It involved books. Specifically, the
recently discovered unpublished manuscripts of
the late horror author Alistair Pendleton.

"Come on, Jaden," Carlos said. Jaden was
staring at his sister's old electronic tablet and had
fallen behind. "What's the hold-up?"

"Sorry, boss man," Jaden said. "Just watching
some clips of the Ghost Grabbers in action."

He showed the tablet to Carlos. On it was
Jaden's favorite web series, *Ghost Grabbers*.

"I can't wait to see the Ghost Grabbers up
close and personal at the library tonight," Jaden
gushed. "Can you believe it? Our library! How
cool is that?"

They paused at the next intersection, waiting
for the light to turn green. Traffic zipped along.

"Check out this clip," Jaden said. "This is
from when the Ghost Grabbers visited a haunted
mansion in New Orleans." He waved a hand to
draw the group closer. "You gotta see this."

Carlos sighed. "You know I don't believe in ghosts," he said, checking the stoplight. Still red. "I'm only going tonight because of the display of Alistair Pendleton manuscripts."

"I'm with you there," Keisha said, moving closer to better see the screen. "But I suppose if we're gonna meet these guys, we should know what they're all about."

"Good point," Carlos said. He trusted Keisha's opinion. They were almost always on the same page when it came to solving mysteries. Carlos joined the others as they huddled around Jaden.

"I can't believe we get to spend the night before Halloween with the Ghost Grabbers," Jaden said, bouncing like a kid in a toy store.

"I can't believe Mom convinced them to let us come tonight," Hayden added. The twins' mother worked at the library. "After all, the live event isn't open to the public. Just employees of the Pendleton Library."

"What exactly are we going to see tonight anyway?" Keisha asked.

Carlos explained. "The library's founder was a famous horror author a long time ago. When he died, there was always talk that he had written more stories that no one knew about. Pendleton's grandson — Andrew Pendleton — recently opened his grandpa's safe. He found a bunch of unknown journals and manuscripts inside. So the library is hosting a special exhibit of the manuscripts."

Jaden continued. "And as a publicity stunt, they're bringing in my favorite squad of paranormal experts to do a séance."

"A what?" Keisha asked.

"A séance," Jaden repeated. "They're going to try and contact the spirit of Alistair Pendleton."

"His ghost supposedly haunts the library," Hayden added.

"Oh, brother." Keisha rolled her eyes. "Didn't we already go through this whole ghost thing with the *Wagons West!* case?"

"This is different," Jaden said. "We're amateurs. These guys? They're pros. Observe."

He tapped the play button, and the clip of the Ghost Grabbers in action began. On the screen, a man with a thick goatee stood in a sea of black. His face was tinted green because of the camera's night-vision setting. "I'm Dean," the man whispered hoarsely, "And that's Connor behind the camera. We're here at the infamous Delacroix Hotel in New Orleans. It's three o'clock in the morning, and we've been hearing some bumps and noises in the third floor hallway. Come on."

The camera bobbed from side to side as the person wielding it walked with the host. Carlos spotted an EMF meter in Dean's hand. Snoops, Inc. had used the same kind of equipment when searching for a ghost in Fleischman Middle School's theater.

The video played on. Suddenly, Dean stopped. "Did you see that?" He was getting excited. "Oh man, the hair on my arms is sticking up. It's getting so cold in here. Look!"

The camera swung down the hall, showing nothing but darkness. Carlos leaned in closer. Even though Carlos didn't believe in ghosts, the video was entertaining to watch.

Connor zoomed the camera. What looked like the silhouette of a person stood at the end of the hall. "Is that what I think it is?" Dean asked.

"Hey kids! Stop blocking the way!" said an irritated voice. While they'd been watching the clip, the light had turned green. People were brushing past them onto the crosswalk.

"Oops, sorry," Jaden said, passing the tablet back to Hayden, who slid it into her backpack. The four quickly hustled across the intersection.

The Pendleton Public Library was a beautiful old building located across the street from Fleischman Middle School. Large columns lined the front, and a glass dome sat atop the structure. It glinted in the evening sun, casting brilliant streaks of light across the cityscape.

The Snoops walked through the domed lobby of the library, which was filled with hazy orange light. Carlos looked up at a large oil painting hung high on one wall and shivered. It was a portrait of the library's founder, Alistair Pendleton. His beady eyes seemed to glare down and follow Carlos' every move.

Just off the lobby was a smaller room where the exhibit had been set up. The manuscripts and black leather journals were displayed on an old roll-top desk. Red velvet ropes blocked off the desk. A poster beside the exhibit read: *Oh, The Horror! The Unpublished Works of Alistair Pendleton*. Carlos hurried toward the display, as if the books were pulling him like a magnet.

Two ladies stood near the exhibit. One was an older lady named Gladys Nelson. Her wispy beehive hairdo made her look very much like a librarian. The other was Hattie Claybourne. Carlos knew Hattie well. They both shared a love of spooky stories. She always set aside copies of new horror novels Carlos might enjoy.

"I was wondering when you guys were gonna show up," Hattie said.

Carlos smiled. "Got here as soon as we could." He stood by the ropes and peered at the display. There they were. The unpublished manuscripts of Alistair Pendleton. Beside them were a set of leather-bound black notebooks. Many were closed, but one lay open. Tiny scribbled notations filled its pages.

"Pretty cool, huh?" Hattie said with wonder.

Carlos nodded.

"They're one-of-a-kind," she said. "It's amazing. What I wouldn't give to sit and read them all."

Carlos leaned in. "They must be worth a fortune," he said. The red velvet rope stretched as he inched forward.

"They are worth a fortune," boomed a voice from behind him. "And I'd suggest you back away from them immediately, young man."

Carlos, stunned, quickly shuffled back. He turned around on one heel, about to apologize —

And found himself staring into the face of Alistair Pendleton!

CHAPTER 3

GHOST GRABBERS!

"Yikes!" Carlos shouted, jumping back.

Of course, it wasn't the real Alistair Pendleton. Carlos knew that. But the man looked freaky-close to the guy in the painting. It was Andrew Pendleton, the library's current owner, and Alistair's grandson. Both grandfather and grandson had the same beady eyes and long nose. And they both wore the same stuffy suits and bow ties. Unlike the thick hair in

Alistair's painting, however, Andrew had gray hair sprouting from above each ear. A wide swath of it was combed over his balding head.

"Sorry, Mr. Pendleton," a woman's voice said.

Hayden and Jaden's mom had appeared. She looked more frazzled than Carlos had ever seen her before. According to Hayden, she'd been working extra hours to make sure the event and the exhibit were perfect.

Mr. Pendleton stared down his nose at them. "Remember," he said. "I gave my permission for your children and their friends to view the event. But only on the condition that they would remain out of the way."

"Yes, sir." Carlos nodded. "We'll be quiet. It'll be like we aren't even here."

"You guys! The Ghost Grabbers just pulled up!" Jaden yelled. He stood by the door, jumping up and down.

Carlos winced as he saw the angry look on Mr. Pendleton's face. "I'll go talk to him," he said, quickly dashing over to his friend.

"Carlos, they're right outside!" Jaden shouted. Carlos placed a finger to his lips and shushed him. "Dude, chill," he said. "Your mom and I just got scolded by Mr. P., so keep your voice down."

Carlos pulled Jaden to the corner of the lobby, where Hayden and Keisha joined them. They watched as two men entered the library carrying large black plastic cases.

"It's really them," Jaden whispered. He opened his mouth to shout at the newcomers, but Carlos clamped a hand over it.

"Keep your cool, man," Carlos whispered.

The first man was instantly recognizable. It was the guy from the video they saw earlier — Dean, if Carlos remembered correctly. Dean was large, with a barrel chest and a trim goatee. A fedora hat was balanced on his head. The second guy must have been Connor, who'd been behind the camera in the video. Connor was a slight man whose flannel shirt hung off his frame. A *Ghost Grabbers* baseball cap sat crookedly and flat-brimmed on his mop of hair.

"Thank you so much for coming," Mrs. Williams said as she approached Dean and Connor. "Did you find the hotel rooms suitable?"

"They were great," Dean said, scoping out the library. "Thanks for booking it for us." He nodded at the oil painting. "Is that Old Man Pendleton?"

"Yes," Mr. Pendleton said sharply as he strode over to join them. "That *old man* is my grandfather."

"No disrespect," Dean said with a smile. He offered Mr. Pendleton his hand to shake. "We're honored to be here. Would you give us a tour of the place?"

"Mrs. Williams will see to your every need," Mr. Pendleton said before striding away.

"Nice guy," Carlos heard Dean mutter under his breath.

"Wow," Jaden said, coming up and quickly shaking the large Ghost Grabber's hand. "Dean and Connor. I'm such a big fan. Truly."

"Hey," Dean said. "Always a pleasure to meet a fan."

Hayden, who had come up behind her brother, was digging through her backpack. From it she produced an EMF meter. The meter measured electromagnetic readings, which some believed were a sign of a ghost's presence.

"Excuse me," Dean said, catching Hayden's attention. "You'll have to put that away. All electronics should be silenced during the séance. That cool?"

"Oh," Hayden said, stashing the EMF meter. "Of course. Sorry."

"So . . . where should we set up our gear?" Connor asked.

Mrs. Williams led the men past the exhibit to a stone fireplace that was set into the wall. The fireplace mantle held framed black-and-white photographs as well as a tall crimson vase. Above it hung a smaller, but just as creepy, painting of Alistair Pendleton. The Ghost Grabbers dropped their gear in the corner, and then went out for more.

"So people really think Pendleton's ghost is hanging around this place?" Keisha asked.

"When Alistair Pendleton died," Jaden said, "a lot of his stuff wound up here. Those chairs —" he pointed to a pair of overstuffed chairs by the fireplace, "— were in his study. Some people think his spirit is still attached to his belongings."

"Mom claims she's heard strange noises in the library sometimes," Hayden continued. "Doors closing, changes in temperature."

"Maybe they just need to check the air conditioner," Keisha said.

"Little help here?"

Carlos turned at the sound of the voice. A teenage girl carrying a stack of sound equipment was staring directly at him. She wore tall black combat boots and a plain black shirt. A shock of purple cut through her closely cropped dark hair.

Carlos, who often used his charm and wit to solve mysteries, tried to speak. But he found he'd lost all ability to form words. It was a new experience for him.

"Can you help me?" the girl asked again. A pair of black noise-canceling headphones dangled from the top of the stack in her hands. They were about to fall to the floor.

Carlos scooped up the headphones.

"Awesome," the girl said. "Follow me."

She led Carlos to where Dean and Connor had stacked their cases and placed the sound equipment beside them. She then took the headphones. "Thanks," she said, smiling at Carlos. He caught a hint of peppermint on her breath, and his heart suddenly hammered in his chest.

"No . . . no problem," he said, flustered. He scurried away, his ears burning hot.

"I can't believe you talked to one of them," Jaden said as Carlos rejoined the Snoops.

"Who is that girl?" Carlos asked.

"Natalie," Jaden said. "Connor's little sister. She runs the sound equipment for them mostly."

"She's . . ." Carlos wanted to say pretty, but couldn't finish the thought.

Keisha elbowed him in the ribs. "Look at this," she said. "Our fearless leader, tongue-tied and full of fear . . . over a girl."

"Shut it," Carlos said.

After the Ghost Grabbers had set up their cameras and other equipment around the wooden table, Mrs. Williams led them on a tour of the library. She spoke about Alistair Pendleton's work, life, and death. When they reached the new exhibit, Hattie Claybourne took over, describing and showing Pendleton's journals and manuscripts.

By the time the tour was complete, darkness had swallowed the sunlight from the glass dome above. Electric lamps cast the library in a hazy yellow glow. Carlos had never been in the building after dark before. He had to admit that the place was pretty creepy.

Dean sat at the table and ran his meaty hands along the wooden surface. "All right," he said. "Let's get this séance started."

CHAPTER 4

THE SPOOKY SÈANCE

"Sound check . . . one . . . two . . . three . . . "

Natalie, wearing the oversized headphones, gave Dean a thumbs-up. She stood near one camera. Connor stood by the other camera, near the fireplace. He toggled a few buttons, watched, then whispered, "And . . . we're live."

Dean waved. "Greetings, all of you watching online. And an early Happy Halloween. I hope you're ready for a spook-tacular experience, because we've got a doozy of an event planned for you tonight."

"This is so amazing," Jaden whispered. The Snoops — alongside Mrs. Williams, Gladys, and Hattie — stood out of the way. Mr. Pendleton was in his office; it was obvious he wanted nothing to do with the séance.

"Welcome to the Pendleton Public Library," Dean continued. "Tonight, live and streaming across the globe, *Ghost Grabbers* will attempt to contact the spirit of its founder — famous horror author Alistair Pendleton."

As Dean filled viewers in on the details, Carlos found his eyes drifting toward Natalie. She watched the small screen of her camera, zooming its lens, biting her bottom lip in concentration.

Dean stopped speaking, casting the whole library in silence. Four electric lanterns that simulated candlelight had been placed on the table. All of the other lights in the room had been turned off. The fake candlelight flickered and danced across Dean's face and on the library walls.

Dean placed his palms on the table and closed his eyes. From what Carlos knew, a séance involved people sitting around a table holding hands. This was a little different, but still unsettling.

They sat in silence for an uncomfortably long time before Dean spoke. "Alistair Pendleton," he said. "Are you present this evening?"

Carlos' eyes darted around. He didn't see anything out of the ordinary. When he glanced at the oil painting above the fireplace, goose bumps cascaded down his arms. In the dim light, Alistair Pendleton's eyes looked even more frightening.

"If your spirit is with us, Mr. Pendleton, please show yourself," Dean said. His voice was calm and soothing. "We're not here to harm you. We just want to speak with you."

Carlos, skeptic that he was, had to stifle a laugh. Dean was taking this way too seriously. Almost like he truly believed a ghost would appear . . .

. . . and then the table shook!

Dean, with both hands flat on the table, remained calm. The wooden table rattled back and forth a bit, shaking the lanterns and nearly knocking them over.

"Whoa," Jaden whispered.

"Did you get that?" Dean asked Connor. The cameraman nodded vigorously.

"Folks," Dean continued, excitement creeping into his voice, "I don't know if you saw that at home, but we've definitely got some spirit action."

Carlos felt a hand on his arm. He looked over and saw Hayden grabbing it. Her eyes were wide with fright.

"It's all right, Mr. Pendleton," Dean resumed. "If you'd like to show yourself to us, or send us a message, we are here for you."

For a moment, nothing happened. But then the lanterns flashed brighter for a second, and then grew dimmer.

"Look!" Jaden cried out.

Across the room, a shape emerged from the shadows. It looked human, with arms hanging down and legs blending into the darkness.

"We've contacted his spirit!" Dean said, pointing at the shadow.

"It's the ghost of Alistair Pendleton!" Hayden said, fear filling her voice. Carlos felt her grip on his arm tighten.

Carlos was mesmerized by the sight. Could it be? Could Alistair Pendleton's ghost be real?

Everyone's attention was focused on the ghostly shape. It was the craziest thing Carlos had ever seen. The shape on the wall raised one arm, then the other, like it was reaching out for them.

And then . . .

The fake candlelight lanterns on the table all flashed and blinked out at once, throwing the whole room into dark chaos!

"AHH!" he heard Hayden scream.

"What's going on!?" Keisha shouted.

"Everyone keep calm," Dean ordered them.

As Carlos' eyes adjusted to the darkness, he reached for his phone. It had a flashlight app on it. His hands were shaking in fright.

"This is unreal," Jaden said.

"Someone hit the lights," he heard Mrs. Williams say.

Long seconds passed before Carlos got his flashlight app working. He swung the beam around and saw the other Snoops next to him. Dean was still seated at the table. Connor was behind the camera; its recording light still glowed red.

Mrs. Williams used the light from the phone to find the wall switch and flick it on.

The room was once again cast in hazy light.

"The ghost is gone," Jaden said, pointing to the wall where the spirit had shown itself. It was nothing but bookshelves and paint again.

"That's not the only thing that's gone," Mrs. Williams said. She was standing beside the exhibit. "Alistair Pendleton's manuscripts are missing!"

CHAPTER 5

SNOOPS IN ACTION

"Where could they have gone?" Keisha asked, arms crossed.

"It's not like the manuscripts and journals could just . . . disappear on their own," Hayden said.

"Unless . . ." Jaden bit his lip, mulling over whether or not he should say what he was thinking. Then, unable to hold it in, he said it anyway, "Unless Alistair Pendleton's spirit took them."

It had been an hour since the séance. The Snoops were huddled in the library, watching as two police officers questioned the people in the room. One of the officers, a tall thin man with a large mustache, jotted notes in a small spiral book. The other was shorter but more muscular. She asked the questions. The officers had already done a search of the area. They'd looked high and low but had not found any of the manuscripts or journals.

"That's ridiculous," Keisha said. "You really think a ghost stole them?"

"Maybe he was upset," Jaden said. "He didn't like us reading all his personal stuff, so he vanished with his journals. I mean, Hayden doesn't like it when I read her diary."

Hayden scowled. "Wait, you read my diary?" she said.

"Um . . . no?" Jaden quickly continued. "We were all here in the room. We all saw the same thing. That shadow was the spirit of Alistair Pendleton. Right?"

"We saw . . . something," Carlos said. "Which means it's up to Snoops, Inc. to figure out exactly what it was."

"How are we gonna investigate this?" Keisha nodded at the two cops, who were now speaking to Mrs. Williams and Mr. Pendleton. The library owner was beyond angry.

"We'll have to be careful," Carlos said, "but I definitely think this weird night just turned into a case for Snoops, Inc." He had gone into detective mode. "We need to get close to the exhibit and check it out. We have to see if the cops missed anything strange."

Snoops, Inc. had worked with the city's police before, bagging criminals and calling it in when necessary. But they didn't know anyone on the force personally. And if the cops here caught them messing with a crime scene, their investigation would be over before it started.

"Assuming someone did take the manuscripts," Keisha said, "you know what that means?"

"It means that someone in this room right now is a thief," Carlos replied.

"Or a ghost," Jaden added.

Carlos sighed. "Keisha and I will check out the display. Hayden, you and Jaden run interference."

"Roger that." Hayden snatched out a handful of plastic bags from her backpack and passed them off to Carlos. "Here, take these, in case you find a clue."

"You just carry those around in your backpack all the time?" Jaden asked.

Hayden nodded. "I'm always prepared."

"Those journals were my grandfather's!" Mr. Pendleton shouted, drawing everyone's attention. He was yelling at Hayden and Jaden's mom. "You left them unattended, and now they're gone."

"And where were you during the robbery?" the police officer asked.

"In my office, away from this stunt," Mr. Pendleton said, glancing at the Ghost Grabbers.

"Mom!" Hayden ran toward the group of adults, pretending to be panicked. "I'm scared."

"Me too," Jaden said, following her. "What if the ghost comes back?" He turned back and gave a huge wink.

"Subtle," Keisha muttered.

While the twins were keeping the police occupied, Carlos and Keisha snuck over to the display. "We have to be quick," Carlos said as they searched near the roped-off desk. "No time to — "

"Got something," Keisha whispered.

"Really? That *was* quick." Carlos was amazed at Keisha's knack for finding clues.

Keisha was kneeling and staring at the carpet. Near one leg of the roll-top desk was what looked like a small, purple disc.

"What is that?" Carlos asked.

Keisha shrugged. "Sure looks out of place though, right?"

"Totally." Carlos took one of the plastic bags and plucked the strange purple item off the carpet. He zipped the bag shut and slid it into his pocket.

"We should check out the area where the ghost was spotted next," Carlos suggested.

"Good idea," Keisha said.

Carlos looked over his shoulder. The twins were still speaking to the cops, gesturing wildly to hold the adults' attention. He and Keisha moved to the table and fireplace area.

A quick scan of the floor offered no further evidence. Carlos checked the wall where the spirit had appeared. He still didn't believe in ghosts, but he did feel slightly unsettled in the area.

As he moved to investigate the fireplace and mantle, a voice behind him hissed, "Psst!"

Carlos jumped. If his breath hadn't caught in his throat, he almost certainly would have yelped out loud.

Nearby, the Ghost Grabbers were packing up their equipment in plastic cases. Natalie had been watching Carlos and Keisha, though. She stowed a tripod in a long case and approached them.

"Hey. What's up with you guys?" Natalie asked. "Are you junior detectives or something?" she added, jokingly.

"We . . . um, yeah." Carlos still didn't know how to act around the girl. He tried to smile, but it felt forced and unnatural.

"Oh," Natalie said. "Really?"

"Snoops, Incorporated," Keisha said, taking charge. She drew a business card out of her pocket. It featured an image of a magnifying glass along with the words:

__Snoops, Incorporated__
__No case too small . . .__
__we solve them all!__

Below their name, a phone number and email were listed, as well as an address. "Cool," Natalie said, pocketing the card. She looked at Carlos, impressed.

He turned to walk away, and ran right into the table. "Oof!"

"You okay, Sherlock?" Natalie asked with a smirk.

"Fine," Carlos said, embarrassed and not looking back.

"Are we clear to leave?" Dean asked the officers. "I'd like to get to the hotel and check the live stream's comments online. I'll bet they're going nuts over tonight's footage. It's gonna go viral for sure."

"That should be fine — as long as you remain there until the manuscripts are recovered," said the second officer.

"But we've got a Halloween gig upstate," Connor countered. "It's at an old abandoned mental institute."

"Not anymore," the officer said with finality.

The grumbling Ghost Grabbers agreed to stay at the hotel. As they carried their cases to the van, Natalie looked over at Carlos and said, "Catch 'ya later, private investigator."

Carlos stammered, "Heh. Catch 'ya . . . too. Um . . . bye."

After the Ghost Grabbers and police officers left, the library grew very quiet and Mrs. Williams approached the Snoops. Her eyes were red, and she looked like she could curl up and fall asleep right there on the floor.

"It's late," she said to the junior sleuths. "You should all head home."

"What about you, Mom?" Hayden asked.

"I'm going to be here a while longer," she said. "Text me when you get home, so I know you're all safe."

Carlos wished the Snoops could stay longer and investigate the library more thoroughly. He had a feeling the manuscripts were still close. But it was obvious they weren't going to get that chance.

Not tonight, anyway, he thought.

CHAPTER 6

CONJURING up SUSPECTS

The four young detectives bundled up and left the library. The temperature outside was colder now after the sun had set. Carlos zipped up his coat and blew into his hands to warm them.

"It's so spooky out here," Hayden said, looking up at the nearly full moon.

"Not as spooky as it was in there tonight," Jaden said.

"I'm ready for a good night's sleep," Carlos said. "After some rest, we can tackle this mystery and find those manuscripts."

"Good call," Keisha said.

The quartet walked down the cement steps of the library. As they did, a voice drifted through the air. ". . . library is going to close . . ."

"What was that?" Jaden asked.

Carlos placed a finger to his lips. A window at the front of the library was cracked open. The voice was coming from there. Carlos slipped beneath the window to hear better.

". . . don't care about the manuscripts." The voice was recognizable.

"Mr. Pendleton," Jaden whispered.

"Will insurance cover the theft?" Mr. Pendleton was asking. It sounded like he was talking to someone on the phone. "Because I could use that money to open an exhibit that isn't about my grandfather — one that people would actually visit. And I wouldn't have to deal with ridiculous ghost hunters at all. Ugh."

Carlos knew that Alistair's grandson wasn't a fan of the séance. He wasn't in the room during the blackout, and was quick to blame someone else for the theft. *Could Mr. Pendleton have stolen the manuscripts himself?* Carlos thought.

It looked like the Snoops had their first suspect for this new mystery.

"What are you kids doing?" a voice asked.

Carlos peered out from the bushes. Hattie Claybourne and Gladys Nelson stood on the sidewalk. They stared quizzically at the four young detectives.

"Oh, uh . . ." Jaden said.

"Hayden thought she dropped something," Carlos said, thinking fast. "We were trying to find it."

"Here it is!" Hayden said. She held a grape sucker in her hand. "It was in my backpack."

"Mystery solved!" Jaden exclaimed, chuckling nervously.

57

The Snoops stepped out of the bushes. They could no longer hear Mr. Pendleton on the phone. Carlos hoped the library owner hadn't heard them talking outside his window.

"I can't believe the manuscripts are gone," Hattie said. "And we probably saw a ghost tonight. It's like something out of an Alistair Pendleton novel."

Carlos nodded. "*The Macabre Mansion.*"

"Exactly!" Hattie said. "That's the one I was thinking about."

"A wild night indeed," Gladys said with a shake of her beehived head. "My life will now seem positively boring compared to this."

"What do you mean?" Hayden asked.

"Dear, didn't your mother tell you? The day after Halloween is my last day as a librarian. I'm officially retiring."

"Aw, that's sad," Hayden said. "I mean, kind of sad, but also cool. Congratulations."

"Thank you," Gladys said. "I've been shelving books here my whole life." She tapped one hand on the large book bag slung over her shoulder. "It'll be nice to just sit and read them instead."

"Come on, Gladys," Hattie said. "I'll walk you to your bus stop." She reached over and took the bag from the older lady's arm. "Let me carry this for you."

"You're sweet, dear," Gladys said. The two librarians said goodbye and then walked off down the street.

The Snoops went in the opposite direction, heading for home.

* * *

"How do I look?"

Jaden spun in a circle, arms wide. He wore a ragged vest and striped shirt, and in his left hand was an enormous hook. He wore a patch over one eye. A battered black hat rested on his head, and a plastic parrot was perched on his shoulder.

"I'm Ghost Pirate!" He held up an issue of his favorite comic, *Ghost Pirate*, with his good hand. "Arrrrrr ya scared?"

It was late the following afternoon, and the Snoops, Inc. team was gathered at the detectives' headquarters. Snoops HQ was actually a basement storage unit in the apartment building where all four kids lived. Rows of chain-link fence storage lockers lined the basement. Carlos had been given permission to use an empty locker to create a makeshift office.

The detectives were dressed for Halloween. Carlos adjusted the cowl on the Action Man costume his mom had bought for him.

"I must say, your costumes are simply mad!" Hayden said to the group. She was dressed as a mad scientist. Her hair was spiked and sprayed white. She wore a long coat and a pair of oversized glasses. Her costume was so crazy that even Agatha, the stray tabby cat that hung around their office, wouldn't go near her. The cat lay curled up asleep on the file cabinet.

On the desk, in a small pool of light, was the plastic evidence bag with the purple disc in it. Keisha was studying it closely. She was dressed as

an Olympic gymnast in a red, white, and blue gym suit. Fake gold medals hung around her neck.

"What is this?" She poked the bag with one finger, moving the disc inside.

"I've got no idea," Carlos said.

"It must be important," Keisha said. "It was right next to the crime scene."

"And it's our only clue," Hayden added.

"So is everyone just going to ignore the fact that we saw a ghost?" Jaden asked. "A real ghost? *Ghost Grabbers* caught it all on camera!"

"Speaking of that," Hayden said, "I rewatched the live feed from the séance last night." She sat in the lumpy desk chair; it groaned and squeaked under her weight. Pulling the chair up, she began typing on the keyboard of the office's ancient, wheezing desktop computer. When she was satisfied, she spun the monitor around for the others to see. "Here it is," she said. "Check it out."

She hit play, and footage from the camera that Connor had operated at the library began. Dean sat at the table, the lanterns lit around him, making him look spooky. As they watched, the table began to shake. "We've contacted the spirit!" said Dean, pointing, and the camera swung right to capture the human shape in the shadows.

Hayden pressed pause. "Did you guys catch it?"

Carlos shook his head. "Catch what?"

"Right before the camera moves." She replayed the video. Dean pointed and shouted, and Hayden paused it. "There."

"Gotcha," Keisha whispered.

Carlos saw it, too. Caught in the dim light was the outline of a person. The figure's back was to the camera, but it was definitely standing near the exhibit.

"Okay, now we've got something! So the manuscripts didn't just vanish," Keisha said. "But who stole them?"

"Let's run down the suspects," Carlos said. "First, Mr. Pendleton. He was suspiciously absent during the séance. He could have grabbed the manuscripts while we were all watching the light show."

"Plus, we heard him talking to somebody about getting a bunch of insurance money for the missing manuscripts," Keisha added. "And we all know that a suspect's number one motive is almost always money."

"What about Hattie?" Hayden asked.

Carlos was stunned by the suggestion. Hattie was his friend, his book buddy. No way she'd snatch the manuscripts. "What about her?" he asked.

"Hattie's an Alistair Pendleton fanatic," Hayden continued. "All she did was talk about how she wished she could read all the journals. What if she stole them so she could do just that?"

Carlos had to admit that Hayden had a point.

"Okay, so maybe as a start, we scope out the library again," Carlos said. "If the books are still there, then maybe whoever stole them will come back to pick them up."

"And if we get a chance to sneak in and check the place out again, even better," Keisha added.

Jaden raised his hook hand into the air. "Can we at least trick-or-treat on our way over there?" he asked. "I spent some quality time making this costume, dude."

Carlos shrugged. "Knock yourself out."

"All right! Let's go trick-or-treating!" Jaden said.

"You mean solve a mystery," Hayden said.

"That too!" said Jaden.

CHAPTER 7

HALLOWEEN STAKEOUT

"We're still in position," Carlos said into his phone. He and Keisha were seated on a bench across the street from the library. It was closed for the evening, and all the lights were dark, except one — Andrew Pendleton's office.

"Roger that," came Hayden's voice. "We are too. Still nothing." The twins were watching the back door of the library from one block over.

"I'm booored," Jaden said into his own phone.

The sun was setting behind the tall buildings of the city. Long shadows cut through with shafts of orange light were cast across the streets. Kids dressed up as vampires, superheroes, undead brain-eating zombies, and more ran or shuffled down the sidewalk. Bags full of sweets swung from their hands.

"Nice costume, dude," said a passing teenager with a hockey mask, giving Carlos a thumbs-up.

"Uh, thanks," Carlos replied.

After another half-hour of waiting, Carlos was about to call it quits. He had his phone to his ear, ready to call off the stakeout, when the light in Andrew Pendleton's office went out.

"We've got movement," Carlos said. He was instantly alert, his fatigue gone in a sugar rush of adrenaline.

Andrew Pendleton exited the front door of the library. He was carrying a briefcase in one hand . . . and a black notebook in the other!

"He's got one of the journals!" Carlos said.

At least, it looked like one of them. From a distance, it was hard to be sure.

Mr. Pendleton was reading from the book as he walked down the steps, oblivious to the fact that Snoops, Inc. was watching him. Keisha quickly snapped some close-up photos of the library owner with her cell phone.

"So he stole and hid the manuscripts," Keisha said. "He keeps his family heirlooms plus gets the insurance money to cover their theft. It's a win-win for him."

"I wonder if the other manuscripts are in his briefcase?" Carlos said. *But the briefcase looks too small,* Carlos thought. *He'd need a much bigger bag to carry all of them.*

"Wait a second," Jaden said over the phone. "We've got something, guys! It's —"

Carlos muted his phone and buried his face in his candy bag. Mr. Pendleton had looked up at the sound of Jaden's excited voice. Carlos risked a glance and saw the library owner walking away.

"Do you think he saw us?" Keisha asked.

"No clue," Carlos replied. "But we have to follow him."

The two Snoops kept the stuffy maybe-thief in their sight but remained a safe distance away. They reached the end of the block and turned left. Trick-or-treaters were still rushing from building to building. They laughed and cheered and munched on chocolate or bubble gum.

Andrew Pendleton made it to the next intersection. Carlos was about to pick up his pace when —

"Oof!"

He ran right into a trick-or-treater, knocking them both to the pavement.

"Hey! Whaddaya think you're . . . Carlos?!"

Only it wasn't just any trick-or-treater. The pirate on the sidewalk was Jaden.

"Wait a second." Carlos helped his friend to his feet. "What's going on?"

"Didn't you hear?" Hayden was coming up behind her brother. "We told you over the phone. Someone's coming. We were following them."

"And we were following . . . " Carlos trailed off. He searched the sidewalk, but Andrew Pendleton was nowhere in sight. They'd lost him.

"Look!" Jaden pointed his hook to the opposite side of the street. Walking along and carrying a rectangular box with both hands was Hattie Claybourne.

"Hattie?" Carlos couldn't believe it. "She's heading for the library."

"Why is she carrying that box?" Keisha asked.

"It looks big enough to hold a whole bunch of books," Hayden said.

Carlos was confused. He was nearly certain Andrew Pendleton had the books. But now, seeing Hattie with the big box, he wasn't so sure.

"Maybe she hid the manuscripts in the library, and is going to use the box to carry them home," Keisha suggested.

The Snoops followed the young librarian. From a distance, they saw her reach the top of the steps, balance the box on one hand, and remove a key from her purse.

She looked in each direction before slipping inside the building.

"Come on!" Carlos was on the move, running briskly across the street. His Action Man cape billowed heroically in the wind.

The front door was still unlocked. Carlos quietly opened it and the pint-sized detectives slipped through. The only light was the bluish moonlight glowing through the glass dome.

Carlos saw Hattie near the fireplace. The box was still in her hands. The four detectives carefully slunk forward. Maybe Hattie would lead them right to the missing manuscripts.

Thunk!

Jaden's plastic parrot had fallen off his costume to the library floor.

"Oops," Jaden said.

Hattie turned to see what had caused the noise and wound up face-to-face with a superhero, a ghost pirate, a gymnast, and a mad scientist.

She unleashed a blood-curdling scream.

AAAHHHGG!

THUNK

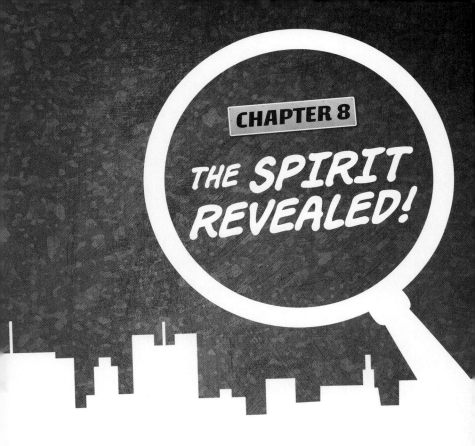

CHAPTER 8

THE SPIRIT REVEALED!

The startled librarian backed away at the frightening sight of the costumed detectives. She first hit the table, and then struck the fireplace mantle. As she stumbled, the box flew out of her hands, sailed through the air, and landed on the wooden floor. With a sickening *Splut!* sound, the lid flipped up, spewing out large clumps of cake and frosting.

A crimson vase on the mantle swayed back and forth, about to topple over. Hattie reached out to grab the vase and keep it from falling. As she did, something fell to the floor and skittered under the table.

With the vase saved, the librarian turned her attention back to the mess on the floor. The box didn't contain the missing manuscripts. Instead, it had held a large sheet cake.

"What are you kids doing here?" Hattie asked.

Carlos stepped forward. "We're so sorry, Hattie," he said. He removed the cowl of his Action Man costume.

"Let me guess," she growled. Carlos had never seen her this angry before. "You're trying to figure out what happened to Alistair Pendleton's manuscripts, so you snuck into the library to find them. Right? Wait . . . were you following me?" Hattie asked.

"Yes," Carlos said. Hattie opened her mouth to uncork a tirade at him, but Carlos cut her off. "It was only because you were sneaking into the library. We thought maybe you had the box so you could carry the manuscripts out in it."

Hattie pointed down at the mess. "Clearly that wasn't the case."

Carlos knelt and began picking up pieces of cake. Part of the cake was still intact. In frosted letters, he could read: Happy Ret . . . ent, Glad . . .

"This was a retirement cake for Gladys, wasn't it?" Carlos asked quietly.

Hattie knelt beside him. "Yeah. Tomorrow is her last day. So I bought a cake and brought it over tonight to surprise her in the morning."

"And we ruined it," Carlos said. "I'm sorry."

"Come on, it's not that bad." Jaden knelt beside Carlos and scooped cake off the floor. "See?" He speared a hunk with his pirate hook and ate it. "Mmm . . . floor cake."

"Gross," Hayden said, wrinkling her nose at her brother.

Keisha got some paper towels and the girls joined in the cleanup effort. As they wiped cake goo off the floor, Keisha suddenly stopped.

"What's that? Hey Carlos, slide me your phone." He did as she directed. Keisha flicked on the flashlight app and shined it under the table.

Lying on the floor was a small black cube. The device was sleek and appeared to have a lens on one side of it.

"Is that a camera?" Hayden asked. She pulled a plastic bag from her pack, and Keisha used it to pick up the cube.

"I dunno," Keisha said. "Could be. Like, a security camera?"

Hattie shook her head. "The library doesn't have any. Mr. Pendleton refuses to spend the money on a decent security system."

Carlos ducked beneath the table. He grabbed his phone and shined the light at the underside of the table. The beam of light had caught something. "That's strange," he whispered.

Carlos noticed what appeared to be scuff marks in one small area. It was probably nothing. But when solving a mystery, Carlos knew that every clue was important. He snapped a photo.

When they were out from under the table, Keisha passed the device to Hayden. She studied it closely. "It could be a camera," she said. "But I've never seen anything like it."

"I think it fell from the mantle," Jaden said. "When . . . you know . . ." He mimed Hattie fumbling around and dropping the cake.

"We should take this back to HQ and get a better look at it," Hayden said.

"That's cool," Hattie said. "I'll just . . . go buy another cake."

Carlos tried to flash her a smile, but felt super guilty about it. "Hey. The new Gordon Price novel, *Alone on Planet Earth*, is coming out next month. I'll buy you a copy. Deal?"

Hattie nodded and smirked. "Deal."

From somewhere in the back of the library, footsteps creaked. The sound echoed loudly in the quiet space. The quartet of Snoops spun. Was someone else there with them?

"Hello?!" Carlos called out into the darkness. There was no response.

They waited a minute. Two. Three. There were no other sounds.

"Come on," Carlos said. "Let's get home."

* * *

A grape sucker danced from one side of Hayden's mouth to the other. She sat at the Snoops HQ desk, the office's desk lamp trained on the device Keisha had found. She was trying hard to figure out exactly what it was.

Meanwhile, Carlos pondered over the photos he and Keisha had snapped. The photo of Andrew Pendleton was slightly blurry. "Could that really be one of his grandpa's missing journals in his hand?" Carlos whispered.

"Maybe," Keisha said.

"First thing tomorrow, we're gonna head back to the library to ask him a few questions," Carlos declared.

"And eat more cake!" Jaden vowed. He'd already eaten half his Halloween candy. How he wasn't groaning with a stomachache was a mystery none of them could solve.

"Guys, look," Hayden called. She held a tiny screwdriver in her hand, and was lifting a flap on one side of the device. "I think I figured it out."

She leaned close, used the screwdriver, and pressed a button.

At first, nothing happened. Then the shadows in the office seemed to swirl and grow. From them a tall, towering specter appeared.

"*IT'S THE GHOST!*" Jaden shrieked.

CHAPTER 9

WE ARE NOT ALONE . . .

"Relax, dummy," Hayden said. She passed a hand in front of the device on the desk, and the spirit in the room winked off and on.

"It's a projection," Carlos said.

"Yep." Hayden clicked off the device, and the spirit disappeared. "Someone planted the device on the mantle and turned it on remotely during the séance."

"So all of our attention would be focused on the ghost while they stole the manuscripts," Keisha said. "Dang, that's clever."

"But who would do something like that?" Jaden asked.

"Sure doesn't seem like something Andrew Pendleton would do," Carlos said.

"But if it's not him or Hattie —" Keisha began.

CRASH!

The sound of toppling boxes rumbled through the storage area.

Someone — or some *thing* — was in the basement with them!

"Hello?!" Just like at the library, Carlos called out into the darkness.

And just like at the library, there was no reply.

The noise had probably come from one of the apartment building's residents who'd stopped down to visit their storage unit. Nothing unusual at all. At least, that's what Carlos told himself.

A lump formed in his throat, making it hard for him to repeat, "Hello?!"

Despite wearing a superhero costume, he was feeling anything but super.

"I'm sure it was just Agatha," Jaden said, gripping his pirate hat and twisting it in his hands.

Poking her head out from under the desk, Agatha meowed, trotted over, and brushed up against Jaden.

"Okay," Jaden said. "Not Agatha."

Carlos crept forward, stepping into the storage room hallway. The other Snoops followed close behind. *Maybe something just fell,* Carlos thought. It happened from time to time. A box probably toppled off a shelf. *Yeah, that had to be it.*

Fluorescent lights hung from the ceiling, casting everything in the area into a shade of pale green.

"Is somebody here?" Carlos asked. The four friends stepped forward as one, moving slowly.

At the end of the hall, a shadow appeared. Dark. Billowy. Human-shaped — and definitely not at all a projection. Carlos' heart lodged itself in his throat.

"Okay . . . now it's a ghost!" Jaden cried.

The specter lunged forward, raising its arms at them.

"Run!" Jaden grabbed Carlos' arm and pulled him back. The four Snoops raced back down the hall, past their office to the end of the row. The specter chased after them. They rounded the corner, found an unlocked storage unit, and ducked inside. Then they crouched in the dark, out of sight —

Except for the sea of tiny eyes that were staring at them!

The storage unit they'd ducked into belonged to Mr. Heckles, who collected ventriloquist dummies. The creepy puppets hung by strings through the entire space. Their unblinking eyes glared down at the Snoops; their grins felt menacing, mocking.

The four detectives huddled there for several long moments. The specter was silent, as if it wasn't there. It did not find them; in fact, it seemed like it wasn't after them at all.

Finally, Carlos crawled to the unit's door and looked out.

Nothing.

"The coast is clear," he whispered.

Cautiously, the detectives made their way back to their office. They were alone again in the basement. Whatever had been chasing them had disappeared.

"What *was* that?" Jaden asked. He released the death grip he had on his wrinkled pirate hat and placed it back on his head.

Carlos walked the hall to the basement door, where the ghost had appeared. The door was cracked open.

"Carlos!" Hayden hollered.

He hurried back to the office. "What?"

She pointed at the desk, and the empty pool of light. "It's gone," she said.

"The projector." He slammed a fist into his open palm. "Whoever chased us away was after it."

"Because they left it at the library," Keisha said. "But how did they know we have it?"

Carlos thought back to the creaking footsteps they had heard at the library. "Whoever it was saw us find it," he said. "The thief was there when we scared Hattie."

Frustrated, Carlos opened his flashlight app and searched the hall. If it wasn't a ghost, the thief must have left footprints. Something. Anything.

That's when he saw it. Another of those strange purple discs lay on the cement floor. This one had been stepped on, though. Half of it had been ground to a powder.

Carlos crouched next to it. Instead of using a plastic bag to pick it up, he simply plucked it off the ground with two fingers. He lifted it to his nose.

With one sniff, the entire mystery suddenly began to make sense.

"Guys," he said. "I think I know who's responsible for everything."

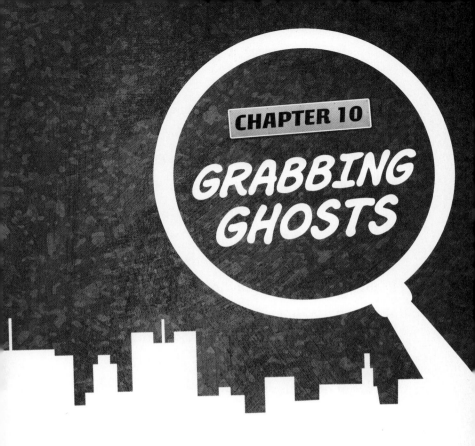

CHAPTER 10

GRABBING GHOSTS

It was past curfew on Halloween, but that wasn't going to stop Snoops, Inc. Carlos had shared his theory with his partners, as well as the answer to the purple disc puzzle. Afterward, the group had quickly gathered their things and picked up some necessary supplies. They were still wearing their Halloween costumes.

Now, Carlos and Jaden secretly crouched behind a bus stop bench to keep watch on the building across the street. As Carlos checked his watch, Hayden came running up, backpack in hand.

"Keisha's set and ready to go?" he asked.

"Yep," Hayden replied

"How about your microphone?" Carlos asked.

From her backpack, Hayden pulled out her parabolic microphone. "All set," she said.

Carlos took a deep breath, dialed a number on his phone, and listened to it ring. When the person on the other end answered he said, "I know you stole the Pendleton manuscripts. I'm heading to the library with proof, and I'm about to call the police."

Then he ended the call before the other person could respond.

"Are you sure about this?" Jaden asked. He'd been the only Snoop to question Carlos' claim.

"I'm positive," Carlos said. "Here we go."

Across the street, the front door of the building burst open. A person came thundering out . . . followed by two others.

Carlos plugged in a set of headphones split off of Hayden's. She pointed the microphone at the parking lot across the street, where it picked up the sounds of a very heated conversation.

"I thought you grabbed the projector," Dean said as the Ghost Grabbers reached their white van.

Natalie threw up her hands. "I did," she said. "Scared the little snots witless. They thought I was a ghost and ran. Then I took it from their so-called office. I don't know how they figured out we stole the manuscripts."

"I knew we should have left town," Connor said.

"Don't you get it?" Dean asked. "If we had vanished, the police would have pegged us as the thieves right away."

"Gotta hand it to the little P.I.," Natalie added. "He's good."

Despite the situation, Carlos couldn't help blushing at the compliment.

"We got what we need?" Carlos asked.

Hayden nodded.

"On to phase two," Carlos said.

He stood up, walked to the bus stop, and stepped up onto the bench. "Boo!" he shouted.

The Ghost Grabbers all turned.

Carlos placed his hands on his hips. His cape billowed in the breeze. He held his chin high and said, "Come and get me!"

Dean, seething with anger, spotted him first. "Hey!" he shouted. He broke into a run, barreling across the parking lot.

"See you guys in a bit," Carlos said to the twins. The Snoops split up. Carlos ran down the block, and easily outpaced the ghost hunter.

A horn honked, and Carlos peered quickly over his shoulder. Connor was driving the *Ghost Grabbers* van and had stopped to pick up Dean.

Oh boy, Carlos thought. He knew the city like the back of his hand. It wasn't far to the library, and he knew he could get there quickly. He just hoped it would be fast enough.

Carlos made a quick turn and ran down an alley. He leapt over a fallen trash can, dodged a parked bike, and broke out onto the next block.

The glass dome of the library gleamed like a beacon over the top of the building in front of him. He was a block away. Close. His lungs burned as he ran, sucking in cold air with each breath.

Screech!

The *Ghost Grabbers* van rounded the corner. Carlos sped up, dashing down another alley.

He made it safely to the library. He bounded up the steps. Thankfully, the door was unlocked. He hurried inside, leaving the door open.

Carlos stopped and waited by the table, watching the open door. It was only a matter of time before . . .

Dean burst in. He scanned the room. "Where are the others?"

"Not here," Carlos said.

"You're alone?" Connor and Natalie entered the library, leaving the door open behind them.

Carlos nodded. "Not for long, though."

"You're bluffing," Dean said. "You don't have any proof we took the Pendleton manuscripts."

"Don't I?" He pointed at the wall where the spirit had appeared. "I've got a photo of the projector you used to make Pendleton's supposed ghost appear at your fake séance," he explained.

"And you think that's proof?" Dean scoffed. "Think the police will believe you?"

"They will when I tell them the whole story," said Carlos.

"I'm curious," Natalie said, sitting on the table. "What *is* the whole story?"

Carlos took a deep breath and explained. "I'm guessing you're hurting for ratings," he said.

"We are not," Connor argued, but Carlos could tell that the comment had struck a nerve.

"What better way to boost ratings than with a successful séance?" Carlos asked. "And having a robbery happen at the same time? Well that's just icing on the cake."

Carlos was in his element, and this time he had no problem finding the right words to say. He looked at Dean. "First, you used something propped on your knee to make the table shake. I found scuff marks under the table."

Carlos next turned to Natalie. "Then, when everyone was focused on the ghost projection, Natalie used a remote to cut the lantern lights."

Turning back to Dean he said, "When everything went dark, she snuck over and snatched the manuscripts from the exhibit while you and Connor were both on or near the camera."

"Me?" Natalie feigned shock. "Why would you think I could do such a thing?"

"Mints," Carlos said. "Peppermint Shockwave Blast, to be exact." From a pouch on his Action Man utility belt, he slipped out the plastic bag with the purple disc in it. "I smelled it on your breath when we met," he continued. "After the robbery, I found this on the floor by the case. I found another in our basement office tonight, after the projector was stolen."

"And how do you suppose we could have gotten the books past the cops?" Natalie asked.

"Your equipment cases. I'm guessing they've got secret compartments in them."

No one spoke. For a moment, the room was silent. Then, Natalie began to clap. "Wow," she said. "That . . . well, that was pretty accurate, actually. Don't you boys agree?"

"Money and ratings," Dean said. "That's what it's all about. When both went south, we needed a way to pay the bills. So we rigged the show."

"And your plan was to sell the Pendleton journals?" Carlos asked.

"Once the heat died down," Connor said. "Yeah. Someone would pay a lot for them."

"Of course," Dean took a step toward Carlos. "Now that you know the truth, we'll have to find a way to make you disappear like Pendleton's unpublished books."

"Not so fast." Keisha stepped out of the shadows from the next room. In her hands was a video camera. A collection of wires snaked from the camera. "You guys aren't the only ones who can set up a live feed. Wave and say hello to all your subscribers."

"What the — ?!" Dean's face contorted, turning a deep shade of red.

"Oh, and you're also not the only ones who can sneak into a place and steal valuable manuscripts," Carlos added. He took his cell phone from his utility belt and turned the screen toward them.

"Hi!" Hayden was on the other end, waving. She was inside the Ghost Grabbers' hotel room.

"Wait," Connor said. "How did you know . . . ?"

"Where you were staying?" Carlos smiled.

"Always helps when your mom is the one booking the hotel room," Hayden said. She turned her camera around to show Jaden in his pirate costume. Next to him were the black plastic cases the Grabbers used to carry their equipment. The cases were open, exposing the manuscripts hidden inside.

"Arrrr!" Jaden said. "We found yer treasure!"

"Did you send our recording of these guys from the parking lot to the cops?" Carlos asked Hayden over the phone.

"Yep!" she replied. "They're on the way."

"Come on," Connor said, slapping Dean on the shoulder. "We gotta fly."

"Nice knowing ya, P.I. guy," Natalie said as the trio raced for the front door.

Before they could reach it, though, the heavy wooden door swung closed. It slammed shut loudly — the sound echoed through the library. Dean tried the knob, but it was stuck. The door wouldn't budge.

Sirens wailed outside, and through the windows came pulsing red and blue lights. The police had arrived.

The Ghost Grabbers were busted.

* * *

"I'm just so glad everyone is okay," Mrs. Williams said, hugging Jaden and Hayden.

"Mom, please," Jaden protested. But not much.

The young detectives stood together in the library, watching as police officers handcuffed the trio of Ghost Grabbers.

"Happy Halloween!" Jaden called out to the ghost hunters.

Dean scowled but said nothing as the cops led him outside.

The two police officers who had originally investigated the theft were back. They took the Snoops' statements as other officers brought the cases containing the manuscripts and journals back into the library.

Mr. Pendleton breezed into the library, wearing a suit coat and looking surprisingly relieved. "They've been found?" he asked.

Mrs. Williams nodded. "By Snoops, Inc. You should be proud of these kids."

Mr. Pendleton looked at Carlos and his friends and said, "Thank you. Sincerely."

"Wait a second," Keisha said. "You were pretty cool with the books gone. We heard you talking about wanting to use the insurance money for a different exhibit."

For a moment, Mr. Pendleton was taken aback. Then, he sighed. "I was, and I did," he said. "Until I read this."

He reached into his coat pocket and removed one of the black leather-bound books.

So he was *reading one of the books when we saw him earlier*, Carlos thought.

"My grandfather wrote many things about many subjects — monsters and ghosts and all of the things that go bump in the night. But he almost never wrote about his family," Mr. Pendleton said. "Except for this. I discovered it before we set up the exhibit, and kept it for myself. I was never close to my grandfather. Not until I read this book. It's all about family and love. It's the most cherished item I'll ever own."

A tear, a genuine tear, fought to escape from his eye. Then he saw the remainder of the mess from the spilled cake on the floor and said, "What in the world happened here?" He strode off.

"That reminds me," Jaden said, nodding at the stain. "I wonder if there's any floor cake left. I'm starving."

"Hey, Hayden," Carlos said. "Smart move rigging the front door to slam shut like that. Did you and Keisha have that planned out when you set up the live feed tonight?"

The two girls looked at him, puzzled. "What do you mean?" Keisha asked. "I thought it was the wind."

"Oh. I didn't feel any wind."

"Don't look at me," Hayden said. "I didn't do anything with the door."

Jaden's eyes were wide. "Maybe it was . . . " He pointed up.

Carlos and the others looked at the creepy oil painting of Alistair Pendleton on the wall. The painting stared back down at him.

A shiver passed down Carlos' arms and neck. "Anyone else wanna call it a night?" he asked.

"Yep," the other Snoops said together, and they all began to hurry toward the front door.

THE END

Snoops, Inc. Case Report #005

Prepared by Carlos Diaz

THE CASE:

The night before Halloween, a spooky event at the library became a case of missing manuscripts when the unpublished works of author Alistair Pendleton disappeared!

CRACKING THE CASE:

That night the *Ghost Grabbers* crew tried to contact the spirit of Alistair Pendleton. When a shadowy figure appeared, the lights went out and the manuscripts were snatched!

We had an idea of who the culprits were, but we had no proof. Thankfully, Hayden had just the thing to get what we needed: a parabolic spy microphone.

The microphone uses what's called a parabolic reflector to collect sound waves. They use the same kind of microphones at major sports events. We pointed the dish-shaped reflector toward the suspects to gather the sound from their voices. The reflector then bounced those sounds to the microphone in the center, where it was recorded on Hayden's phone.

By using the parabolic mic we recorded the culprits' conversation, giving us the proof we needed. So it totally helped us to . . .

CRACK THE CASE!_

WHAT DO YOU THINK?

I. Author Alistair Pendleton left behind many unpublished stories and journals. What do you think they contained? What made them so valuable?

2. Jaden is obsessed with *Ghost Grabbers*. Why do you think this is? What is so interesting about the group? Are there any Internet video sites you are interested in?

3. Gladys Nelson is happy to retire, because it means she can spend her days reading. If you could spend all your time reading, what types of books would you choose? Why?

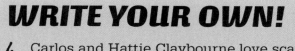

WRITE YOUR OWN!

1. Carlos and Hattie Claybourne love scary stories by Alistair Pendleton. What authors to you love? Try to write a short story in the same style as your favorite author.

2. Andrew Pendleton's feelings about his grandfather changed after reading one of his journals. Write about a time when your opinion of someone changed after getting to know them.

3. Pretend that you are trick-or-treating on Halloween and see something super scary. Write about your imaginary adventure.

GLOSSARY

ADRENALINE (uh-DREH-nuh-luhn)—a chemical the body produces when a person is excited

EVIDENCE (EV-uh-duhnss)—information, items, and facts that help prove something to be true or false

INSURANCE (in-SHUR-uhnss)—a contract between a person and a company to protect against damage or loss of valuable items

MESMERIZE (MEZ-muh-rahyz)—to hold a person's complete attention as if they are hypnotized

PARABOLIC (pair-uh-BOL-ik)—having a curved or rounded shape

PARANORMAL (pair-uh-NOR-muhl)—having to do with an unexplained event that has no scientific explanation

SÉANCE (SEY-ahnss)—a meeting to contact the spirits of the dead

SILHOUETTE (sil-oo-ET)—an outline of something that shows its shape

STAKEOUT (STAKE-out)—a situation in which someone watches a place to look for suspicious activity

ABOUT THE AUTHOR

Brandon Terrell has been a lifelong fan of mysteries, shown by his collection of nearly 200 Hardy Boys books. He is the author of numerous children's books, including several titles in series such as Tony Hawk's 900 Revolution, Jake Maddox Graphic Novels, Spine Shivers, and Sports Illustrated Kids: Time Machine Magazine.

When not hunched over his laptop, Brandon enjoys watching movies and television, reading, watching and playing baseball, and spending time at home with his wife and two children in Minnesota.

ABOUT THE ILLUSTRATOR

Mariano Epelbaum is an experienced character designer, illustrator, and traditional 2D animator. He has been working as a professional artist since 1996 and enjoys trying different art styles and techniques.

Throughout his career Mariano has created many expressive characters and designs for a wide range of films, TV series, commercials, and publications in his native country of Argentina. In addition to Snoops, Inc., Mariano has also contributed to the Fairy Tale Mixups and You Choose: Fractured Fairy Tales series for Capstone.